Odette Elliott

Nightingale News

Five stories about our school

Illustrated by Jacqueline East

To Natasha and Amber with love

Scholastic Children's Books,
Commonwealth House,
1-19 New Oxford Street, London WC1A 1NU, UK
a division of Scholastic Ltd
London ~ New York ~ Toronto ~ Sydney ~ Auckland

Published in the UK by Scholastic Ltd, 1996

ISBN 0 590 13630 5

Typeset by Backup... Design and Production, London
Printed by Cox & Wyman Ltd, Reading, Berks

10 9 8 7 6 5 4 3 2 1

1

Dancing in the Rain

On Friday afternoon at Nightingale School Miss Merryday gave a letter to everyone in Class 1.

"Do you remember the news I told you today about our Arts Week?" she said. "This letter tells your parents all the things they need to know about it."

Jack gave the letter to his mum. As

soon as he got home he forgot all about school.

On Saturday Jack was having a lovely game with his cars when his little sister came in, pointing her toes and waving her arms about. She tripped over two of his best cars.

"Mum! Katie's spoiling everything!" Jack shouted. He looked at his line of cars all knocked sideways and in a mess. Then he looked at his little sister. She stood there in her silly sticky-out dress that she got at a jumble sale. She was rubbing her foot.

"Ow! Jack's cars hurt me! I was dancing!" she wailed.

"Dancing, stupid dancing!" Jack growled. "That's all you ever do – jump around and say you're dancing. You think everybody thinks you're sweet. Well, I don't! Yuk!"

"*You'll* be dancing next week!" said his older sister Natasha, who was sitting watching television. "I heard Miss Merryday talking about it."

She turned to Mum who had come into the room to see what the fuss was about. "Mum, my class is doing acting in the Arts Week. Did you know Jack's class is doing dancing?" she said.

"Good," said Mum. "We'll be coming to see you both at the end of the week. Parents and friends are invited."

"And sisters?" asked Katie, jumping up and down. "Can I see Jack dance?"

"Sisters are stupid!" Jack growled. "So's dancing!"

He picked up his cars and put them noisily into the square biscuit tin he used for a garage and went up to his room to be miserable alone.

"I shall have to think of a plan," he said aloud in his room. "What CAN I do to get out of the dancing?"

Jack lay on his bed with his hands behind his head and stared up at the lampshade in the middle of the ceiling. It was made of paper and was like a blue hot-air balloon. There was a little basket hanging underneath. It was the kind of hot-air balloon that people can travel in. He stared at it for a long time.

Then an idea came to him. He jumped off the bed and smiled broadly as he set his cars out again. This time they would be quite safe from Katie's feet. He hummed to himself and had a lovely afternoon!

At school the next day Jack tried pretending that he had hurt his foot. He had to get out of dancing somehow!

"Look! Miss Merryday! I've hurt my foot. I can't dance!" he said as he hobbled into the classroom.

Miss Merryday only gave a quick look; she was busy helping to put a ribbon back in Daisy's hair. "I'll look in a minute," she said.

Jack hobbled over to show Rosie and Ruth. He waved his foot around. "Can't walk on it so I can't dance today. Probably can't dance all week," he said, trying to sound sorry.

They stared at him but didn't say anything so he went over to Mustapha.

"So aren't you playing out tonight?" was all Mustapha said.

Jack didn't have to answer because Miss Merryday had finished doing Daisy's hair.

"Now show me," she said. "Let's see how bad it is."

Jack hobbled over to the window to show Miss Merryday.

"That's his other foot! And he hasn't even got a bandage!" said Daisy.

Jack stared at her with his most furious look.

"Bother! You'd better sit out for a bit," said Miss Merryday. "I tell you what. You can help me with the music until your foot gets better."

Jack nodded. He wanted to grin but thought he'd better not. Instead he stuck his tongue out at Daisy. He did it when she wasn't looking in case she got him into trouble.

"Right!" said Miss Merryday. "Before we do anything we have to warm up our muscles. You can do any of this, Jack, as long as it doesn't mean using your bad foot."

Miss Merryday put a big box down beside him. It had tambourines and triangles and a drum in it. "There you are!" she said.

"What can we do to warm our hands?" she asked the class.

"Clap," said Chantelle.

"Good! Let's all clap our hands."

Everybody clapped until their hands ached.

"Now our arms. How shall we warm them?" asked Miss Merryday.

"Swing them," said Mustapha.

"Good. Let's swing our arms and take

big steps round the hall, then stop!"

The children swung their arms and took big strides. "I'm being a soldier," said Mustapha.

"I'm in a marching band," said Mary. She pretended to play a trumpet with one hand and swung the other arm very smartly. When Miss Merryday said, "Stop!" they all stopped at once like they were used to doing in PE, but they all bumped into each other because they weren't looking where they were going.

Jack laughed because he was the only one who hadn't moved and didn't get bumped.

"That was silly!" said Miss Merryday. "Eyes in front! Look where you are going."

She waited until everybody was quiet, then said, "March again!"

Everybody marched.

"And STOP!"

Everybody stopped.

"Now listen carefully. Our group and the art group are going to do work about THE WEATHER this week."

Jack groaned. "That's boring!" His words came out louder than he meant. In fact "boring" came out very loud indeed and everyone looked at him.

"Be quiet," said Miss Merryday. "And wait and see!"

Jack looked behind him and pretended that somebody else had spoken. He hummed a little tune to show that he didn't care.

Then he had an idea.

He knew that Miss Merryday could always see him when he was messing about but he thought that he could hide from her behind the piano. She wouldn't be able to see him there. He slid sideways and backwards slowly, slowly until he was out of view behind the piano. It was a bit quieter behind there, but it didn't work!

"Back you come, Jack, where I can see you!" came Miss Merryday's booming voice.

She came over to bring him out and handed him a tambourine.

"You can help us all by shaking this to

make us think it's very windy. Children, when you hear Jack shake the tambourine I want you to whirl away. Pretend you are leaves caught up in the wind. You can go up, down, round and round! Like this. Look!"

Miss Merryday twirled and jumped and so did her necklaces and earrings. Rosie and Ruth giggled but Miss Merryday didn't hear. Suddenly she stopped.

"Let me see you all – now!" she said, breathing heavily.

Jack shook the tambourine. It was fun at first because he could make the children go slower and faster by shaking the tambourine slower or faster. But he didn't think that any of them were much good.

I'd be much better than all of them at whirling! he thought. He had often watched those little seed aeroplanes from the big tree near his house go round and round and he knew *he* could whizz round like them. Or he could have pretended he was a crisp packet being blown round and round by the wind…

"Good! Now you can all sit down for a minute," said Miss Merryday. "Come and have a rest. In a moment I want everybody to find a partner. We'll pretend the sun is coming out. Think hard about the rays of sunshine."

This will be silly, Jack thought to himself. I don't like stupid partner dancing.

Miss Merryday didn't mention any music and Jack was glad. She talked about sunshine and stuff. Then she said, "Stand up now and hold hands with a partner. Show me how far you can stretch away from each other. I want you to be rays of sunshine. Stretch all your body, even your fingers."

Now things were getting more interesting! Jack had never thought that

stretching could be called dance. If he'd
been Mustapha's partner they could have
made the biggest stretch. It was boring
just sitting and watching. There was no
partner for him.

"I'm good at stretching, Miss," he said,
but Miss Merryday didn't hear.

I'll tell her my foot is better at
playtime, he thought.

When they stopped for the morning play he tried to run after her and say that his foot felt better but Miss Merryday shot out of the hall in a big hurry.

Outside in the playground, Jack sulked. "Stupid Arts Week!" he muttered as he kicked an applecore round and round the playground. He didn't even bother to pretend to have a bad foot any more.

After break, Miss Merryday brought the class back to the hall and gathered them all into a circle round her.

"Let's think about the rain now! What is it like when it rains?" she asked. "How do you have to walk when there are big puddles?"

Jack wanted to join in with this and stop doing the music. He liked the sound of walking in puddles and he put his hand up. He was going to say, "Miss, my foot's better," but Miss Merryday chose Mary instead because she was waving her arm in the air as if she was going to burst.

"You have to jump, Miss," she said, "to miss the puddles – or if you've got wellies on you're allowed to splash in the puddles."

"Brilliant!" said Miss Merryday. "Those are two beautiful ideas. Jack – can you take the triangle first and make a little sound for raindrops and then bang the drum for the heavy rain?"

"Miss," he said. "My foot…" but Miss Merryday clapped her hands and said in her extra-loud voice, "Everybody begin!"

Jack dug in the box for the triangle. It was fiddly to strike and he didn't like it much. The next bit – the heavy rain – was better. BOOM! BOOM! He did his part very well.

Jack's drum beat was very loud but the others were useless. They looked frightened of the puddles. He knew that *he* would be able to move so that everyone would feel they were getting splashed! He wondered whether he dared to stop playing and just join in. What would Miss Merryday say?

Just then Jack noticed that Mrs Thompson, the Headteacher, had come out of her room. She was waving to Miss Merryday and trying to attract her attention. She had a note in her hand. Miss Merryday wasn't looking.

"Shall I take the note and give it to her?" Jack asked.

"Would you, please? That would be very helpful," said Mrs Thompson and she gave him the piece of paper and went back into her room.

Now he had an excuse to stop playing. Jack put the drum down and stepped into the middle of the hall to reach Miss Merryday. He took big steps and bent his knees up high. He could almost feel the rain splashing down into the back of his pretend welly boots.

The others were surprised when the beat of the drum stopped and they looked at Jack. Rosie and Ruth giggled and Mustapha stared.

"Amazing!" said Miss Merryday. "Is your foot better already? Everybody look at Jack. See how he is striding along. Try and lift your legs high like Jack. I can almost see the big puddles as he splashes in them!"

She took the note from him and Jack started off again. All the class followed him.

After that nobody mentioned a bad foot and later most of the class took it in turns to help with the music; in fact nearly everyone in the class except for Jack. He stayed in the middle of the hall and joined in everything.

In the afternoon, when his mum and Katie met him at going-home time, Jack said, "Our dancing's not like Katie's dancing at all. It's good. We're doing weather."

He caught up with Mustapha and his brother. "Are you playing out tonight?" he asked.

"Yep," Mustapha answered. "I'll come for you. Okay?"

"Good!" said Jack. He grinned. Today had turned out okay after all.

He turned round to Mum and Katie who were just behind him. "I don't mind if you come and watch me dance at the end of the week," he said. "What I'm best at is DANCING IN THE RAIN!"

2

The New Girl

"We're going in the Home Corner," said Rosie.

"We're dressing up," said Ruth.

Chantelle watched Rosie and Ruth. They always played together. Ruth had put on a big blue hat and she was carrying a big basket. She was pretending to be a lady going shopping.

It was choosing time at the end of the

day. Everyone in the class was busy. Chantelle was the only one in the Book Corner. She was reading a story but she kept looking up to see what the others were doing.

Reading is all right, she thought, but I would rather have a best friend. Then we could choose something to do together.

When Chantelle joined the class at Nightingale School as a new girl, all the other girls already had best friends and nobody needed her to be their best friend.

Sometimes she played with the boys but today there were so many of them building something big that there wasn't room for anyone else. She gave up looking around and concentrated on her book.

Soon Chantelle became so interested in the story she was reading that she didn't hear Miss Merryday call everyone to stop and gather in the Book Corner. She just looked up and there they were, sitting all round her.

Miss Merryday was talking to the class.

"I've got some news," she said. "We have a new girl arriving tomorrow. She is French and she has just come to England to live. She can't speak any English yet, so I want you to be extra good and helpful!"

I wonder if she'll be my best friend? thought Chantelle.

The next day, Mrs Thompson, the Head-teacher, introduced the new girl to the class.

"This is Anne-Marie," she said. "She is joining us at Nightingale. I know you will all be very kind to her. She has come to England to stay with her auntie. She doesn't know any English yet, but I'm sure she will soon learn from you."

Anne-Marie didn't look at anyone. She stood with her head down but Chantelle saw her face and she thought that she seemed very sad.

I wonder why she looks so sad? she thought. She crossed her fingers, thinking, I wish I could be her friend!

Chantelle couldn't believe it when Miss Merryday put a chair for Anne-Marie at the table she shared with Rosie and Ruth.

"You can sit here," Miss Merryday said slowly, showing Anne-Marie the chair. "This is Rosie, this is Ruth and this is Chantelle. They will all help you."

Rosie and Ruth giggled and Chantelle smiled a welcome smile. It felt funny not being able to say anything she could understand.

Anne-Marie just sat down and carried on staring at the table. Chantelle wanted to take her hand when it was time for Assembly but Rosie and Ruth jumped up and each took a hand.

After Assembly Miss Merryday gave everybody in the class some work to do and then she spent quite a long time with Anne-Marie. Miss Merryday could speak a few words of French, but Anne-Marie was so quiet and sad-looking that nobody knew whether she understood or not. Miss Merryday gave her some pictures to colour in. She had written the words underneath in French and English.

Chantelle peeped at the French words but she couldn't read them.

In the afternoon, Anne-Marie was allowed to look at the picture books in the Book Corner while the rest of the class did writing. Chantelle was always quick at doing her work and as soon as she had finished her writing, she asked if she could join Anne-Marie in the Book Corner.

She went and sat on Miss Merryday's chair. It was where Miss Merryday sat when she read aloud to the class. Nobody else was allowed to sit on that chair. She

picked up a book with lovely bright pictures. She thought she would make Anne-Marie smile.

"Miss! Miss!" Daisy said. "Chantelle's sitting on your chair!"

Chantelle didn't listen to Daisy. She opened the book and held it out like Miss Merryday did, to show Anne-Marie the pictures. Slowly, slowly, Anne-Marie lifted up her head. Chantelle pointed to

the pictures just like Miss Merryday did for the class. Anne-Marie did not smile but after a bit she did look at the pictures. Then Chantelle heard Miss Merryday call out in a very loud voice, "Chantelle! Why are you sitting on my chair?"

"I'm showing the new girl a story and she's looking at the pictures, Miss," said Chantelle.

"What a good idea! Well done!" said Miss Merryday.

"Why can't I sit on Miss Merryday's chair? Why is Chantelle allowed to?" grumbled Jack.

Miss Merryday heard him. "Chantelle had a very good reason," she said. "People can only sit on my chair if they have a very good reason. Now get on with your work the rest of you. I want to see some of your best writing."

After story time at the end of the day Miss Merryday asked, "Would anybody else like to sit on my chair another day?"

The children looked at each other and nodded their heads.

"I've had a good idea. I'll let you sit on it if you read aloud to the class. That would be a very good reason for sitting on my chair!" she said.

"I tell you what I shall do," Miss Merryday continued. "Tomorrow I shall pin a piece of paper on the board by my desk and anyone who wants to read aloud can sign their name."

Chantelle was thinking about Anne-Marie and wasn't listening very carefully to Miss Merryday.

The next morning the children stood and looked at the piece of paper Miss Merryday had pinned to the noticeboard. It said:

Put your name below if you want to read to the class :-

"I'm not sitting on that stupid chair if you have to read!" said Jack.

"Why don't you put your name down?" Daisy asked Mustapha.

"I'm not a very good reader," said Mustapha.

"You can all be good readers if you try," said Miss Merryday. "I'll help you to practise reading out loud. So will Mr

O'Connor when he comes to help us. And if you're not ready to read, you can just tell us all about what is in a picture and show the class the picture."

Mary practised reading a story about some children who went on a picnic. (She always liked stories about food.) She was the first person to write her name on the piece of paper. The children crowded round the board as she wrote her name.

Chantelle didn't bother to look. Instead she drew a funny picture for Anne-Marie and gave it to her. She didn't smile but she looked at it for a long time and Chantelle was pleased about that.

Rosie and Ruth had stopped trying to include Anne-Marie in their games because she always looked so miserable. Chantelle was the only one who tried to help her.

Miss Merryday said, "I don't know what I would do without you, Chantelle. You are a great help to Anne-Marie."

But Chantelle sighed. She didn't think Anne-Marie could be called a friend yet. Proper friends smiled and laughed together.

Meanwhile the children in Class 1 were still talking about having a turn sitting on Miss Merryday's chair.

Mustapha loved looking at a big red book about buses. His uncle drove a bus and he knew that if he had to read a book he would choose that one. There were not many difficult words in it and Mr O'Connor helped him to practise reading aloud. At last he felt brave enough and he wrote "Mustapha" on the list.

Soon it was Mary's turn to read. She

was the first person. Some children weren't listening when she started.

"Sit properly!" she said in a voice like Miss Merryday's stern voice. She leaned forward and stared at everyone as crossly as she could.

Chantelle looked at Anne-Marie. She was sitting very straight and properly but she looked as if she were thinking of something miles away with her sad eyes.

When it was Mustapha's turn to sit on the chair and read, he giggled and forgot the words.

Miss Merryday said, "Just start again, Mustapha," and he did. He had to start twice more but in the end he read it all properly.

Soon all the children in the class were busy getting a book ready to read to the class – except for Jack.

"I'm not reading on that stupid chair!" he said again. "You can't make me!"

The only person who did not talk about sitting on Miss Merryday's chair was Anne-Marie. Each day that she came to school she was very quiet and looked sad and hardly learned any words of English. Chantelle began to wonder if she would ever make her smile or if she could ever be her friend.

Then Chantelle had an idea and talked to her granny about Anne-Marie. Chantelle's granny came from an island called Mauritius and she knew some French.

The next day Chantelle came into the

classroom in a hurry. She went straight to the noticeboard and wrote her name down on the list.

"I was the first to sit on the chair," she explained to Miss Merryday and to anyone else who was listening, "but I haven't read to the whole class – only to one person and that's not fair."

She hugged a bag close to her and kept it with her all day. Miss Merryday asked her if she needed any help with reading her story but she said, "No thank you."

When it was Chantelle's turn to sit on the chair, she put the bag on her lap. "I'm going to show you a picture from a book," she said. "It's my granny's book."

Carefully, Chantelle took the picture book out of the bag. She held it up so that all the children could see. "My granny said that when she was a little girl she went to school near this beach." She pointed to a beautiful sandy beach that stretched in a big curve. The sea was a bright blue-green and tall coconut palms rose into a deep blue sky.

"She did all her lessons in French and she told me about her favourite French song. It was called "Frère Jacques". Can I sing a bit of it?" she asked Miss Merryday.

"Certainly, dear," said Miss Merryday.

So Chantelle sang all the words her granny had taught her.

When she finished, all the children in Class 1 clapped except for Anne-Marie, but she sat and smiled and smiled.

It was the first time that Anne-Marie had smiled at school!

Chantelle put her granny's book back in the bag very carefully and jumped down from Miss Merryday's chair.

When she sat down next to Anne-Marie, to her surprise Anne-Marie gave her a little kiss on each cheek.

At the end of the day Chantelle said to her mother, "I'm the only person who has made the new girl smile and I think she's going to be my friend." She thought for a bit and then she added, "I'm going to ask Granny to teach me some French words, then we can play and talk together!"

And she skipped ahead of her mother all the way home. And she had an extra-big grin all over her face!

3

Melodie and the Duck

Miss Merryday looked out of the classroom door down the corridor in both directions. "I'm afraid we can't wait any longer," she said to Mr O'Connor, the class-helper. "If you lead the class, I'll walk with the children at the back."

She turned to the parents who had come to help. "Can you please look after the children in the middle of the line?" she said.

"I *knew* Melodie would be late!" Daisy sighed.

Just then there was a thud thud noise in the corridor and Melodie Miller came running in. She was wearing a long dress, a coat and wellington boots.

Unfortunately she tripped over her dress and fell straight on to Rosie and Ruth who were at the front of the queue.

They fell backwards and in a twinkling six children had all fallen over in a heap. They lay there on top of each other, blinking their eyes.

"Goodness me! What an entrance!" said Miss Merryday.

She and Mr O'Connor pulled the children to their feet. Luckily nobody was hurt.

"Are you all all right?" she asked, inspecting the children.

Rosie and Ruth patted each others' coats to get the dust off and did not answer.

"All right, Miss," the others answered.

"Let's just pause for a moment before we go," said Miss Merryday. "Let's all calm down. Now. Who remembers what we are going to do on our Mystery

Outing? Do you remember what I told you in the classroom?"

"To learn about flowers, Miss," said Chantelle.

"To use our noses, Miss," Jack said, holding his nose between his fingers.

"And our eyes and our ears," added Daisy.

"Good!" said Miss Merryday. "And remember! I shall want to see your best writing and drawing when we get back!"

Some children groaned but Miss Merryday took no notice. She looked at the class. "Stand up nice and straight. We want people to think Nightingale School children look smart. Are we ready to go?"

"Yes, Miss!" the children said in sing-song voices.

"Good! Come with me, Melodie. I think you had better walk with me at the

back. Then you can tell me all about your adventures. Right. Off we go!"

And off they went.

"Pooh! I smell chalk," Jack said as he walked past the blackboard. He wrinkled his nose. Mustapha giggled and had a peep at Miss Merryday to see whether she would be cross, but to his surprise she was smiling.

Class 1 trooped out of the classroom, through the hall, down the steps to the playground, across the playground,

through the school gate and towards the crossing.

As they reached the crossing Jack asked, "Where are we going, Miss? You haven't told us where. I hope it isn't too far. My legs ache when I have to walk."

"I shall pretend I did not hear that," said Miss Merryday. "Your legs don't seem to ache when you want to play football. I've seen you running like the wind! I have already told you that this is a Mystery Outing. We are going somewhere where we shall see lots of flowers and it's quite near here."

As they walked along, Melodie told Miss Merryday her long, complicated story. "First we got up late and we couldn't find my baby brother and then we couldn't find the guinea-pig and we went round to my auntie's and my brother was there in his pyjamas and she had rescued the guinea-pig and then I had to get dressed –"

"Stop! You're making my head go round! Perhaps we'd better think about the outing now and forget about all those adventures!" said Miss Merryday.

Melodie stopped talking and tried to be quiet. She wanted to make Miss Merryday pleased with her.

The class walked past a garage that was selling cars.

Everyone wanted to have a look at the shiny new sports cars. Everyone except Melodie. She walked over to look at some big pink and blue flowers in tubs.

I'll smell those flowers and then Miss Merryday will be pleased with me! she

thought. She buried her nose in the tiny bell-shaped petals. "Mm! Lovely smell. Like my mum's soap!" she said to herself.

She picked two flowers to show Miss Merryday and was just going to tell her that she had used her nose to smell their perfume when Miss Merryday called her. She sounded cross.

"Melodie Miller! Come here at once!" she said. "Did you pick those?"

"They're for you, Miss," Melodie said in a small voice.

"Mm! Nice!" said Mary.

But Miss Merryday wasn't pleased at all. "I thought you children knew that you must NEVER pick flowers that belong to other people!"

Everyone looked at Melodie. Melodie looked at her feet.

Mr O'Connor and the parents made the children form a neat line in twos again and they walked on past a row of shops. Some children walked slowly and looked in the windows.

"Let's hurry and all keep together," said Miss Merryday.

"HOW FAR are we going?" asked Jack. "You STILL haven't told us."

"All right. Since you can't wait until we get there, I'll tell you. We're going to a little park to see the flowers. It's very, very near," said Miss Merryday.

"Where's the park? I don't know a park round here," the children said. "Have you seen a park?" they asked each other.

They walked on past some more shops, then turned a corner and Miss Merryday stood in front of a big iron gate that had a small roof over it. "Stop everyone! This is the entrance to the little park. Haven't any of you been in here?" she asked. "It's a big church garden and it's open for everyone."

"I'm not going in there. It'll be all full of spiders," said Mustapha straight away.

"I will! I'll go in!" said Melodie.

"And me!" said Owen, who hardly ever spoke. He went all red when everyone looked at him. "Flowers are good," he mumbled to himself.

The class turned round past a hedge and there in front of them were beds of beautiful flowers. There were so many different colours!

"Cor!"

"Magic, Miss!"

The children walked slowly along the path towards the flowers.

"We'll stop here. Let's look at the daffodils first," said Miss Merryday. "And remember – just look! Don't pick any!"

The class spread out so that they were standing by the big flower-bed that was shining yellow.

"See the yellow bit in the middle. People say that it's shaped like a trumpet," said Miss Merryday.

"I can't see," said Mustapha, standing on tiptoe.

"There's room here," said Melodie. She stepped quickly to one side but she tripped over something and wobbled, then fell head first right into the bed of yellow daffodils. She had daffodils in her eyes and nose. She heard everybody gasp and felt Miss Merryday and Mr O'Connor pull her up.

"Are you hurt?" Miss Merryday asked.

"Have you got a worm up your nose?" asked Jack.

"Don't be silly, Jack!" Miss Merryday said with a big frown. "If you are not hurt, Melodie, please go and stand by that seat over there. You will be safer away from the flower-beds. You can listen and learn but don't pick anything and don't fall into any more flowers!"

Melodie stood by the seat. She sniffed. "It's not fair!" she said in a wobbly voice. She tried hard to use her ears to hear what Miss Merryday was saying about the flowers. She heard the words "tulip" and "hyacinth" but not much else.

Then she heard a strange kind of "swish-pat, swish-pat" noise coming from behind the bench.

Melodie stopped listening to Miss Merryday and used her ears to follow the strange sound. She walked very slowly. When she reached the hedge by the park gate she saw a little duck. It had a large white polythene bag stuck on its foot. It was trying to shake it off as it walked – "swish-pat, swish-pat".

Melodie got nearer to the duck but it waddled away from her right into the hedge. She wriggled into the hedge until she could just reach the duck. Slowly, slowly she tried to get the polythene bag off its leg but now the bag was also caught on the bushes.

Then Melodie found that she too was stuck! The branches were caught and she couldn't move.

"Help! I'm stuck! I'm here, Miss! Don't leave me!" she called out. There was no reply.

She called again, "Help! Come and find me!" and waited for someone to come. Nobody came.

She wriggled again but she still couldn't get out of the hedge. This time she shouted at the top of her voice,

"He-lp! I'm in the he-dge…! By the ga-te!"

Melodie heard Miss Merryday call out to the class, "Freeze everybody! Turn yourselves into statues and don't move until I've found Melodie!"

Melodie heard Miss Merryday and Mr O'Connor come running up the path. They took hold of her arms and legs and moved the branches gently until she was free. Her arms and legs were scratched but she was brave about it and didn't make a fuss.

Just at that moment the duck worked
its way out of the hedge. It dragged itself
– "swish-pat-swish" – back down the path
towards the class.

Melodie ran after it and gently finished pulling off the bag. Now it was free! The duck looked at her with a beady eye, then flapped its wings and flew away.

The whole class stopped being statues and they clapped and cheered. The parents and some passers-by clapped too.

"That was very kind and clever of you, Melodie," said Miss Merryday. "But please stay where I can see you IF EVER I take you out again!" She sat down heavily on the park bench and wiped her brow with a pink handkerchief.

When they got back to the classroom everybody drew pictures and did some writing. Daisy wrote, "I liked the flowers. Melodie got lost and didn't get told off."

Jack drew a picture of Melodie in the daffodil bed. He wrote: "Miss Merryday found a secret park. I didn't think there was one but there was."

He didn't think he would write about a worm in Melodie's nose, but he drew a pink wriggly one coming along the flower-bed. He showed it to Mustapha and they both giggled.

Melodie sat chewing her pencil because she could not think what to write. At last she had an idea.

"I used my ears to follow the duck. Can I write about it and draw it, instead of flowers, Miss?" she asked.

"Of course!" said Miss Merryday.

Miss Merryday put all the work up on the wall by her desk. The children gathered round to see what everyone had done.

Melodie's story with a picture of the duck flying away was right in the middle. All the children in Class 1 thought that her story was the best –

– and that her picture was lovely!

4

Owen's Special Flower

Owen sighed and looked over to the window. Long lines of rain were falling down the panes. It was still raining! It had been raining all day. They had spent all morning play and all the dinner-time stuck in the hall.

Owen sighed again – a big, noisy sigh. Usually he kept very quiet at school.

Daisy heard him. She tried to spin her

pencil round on the table to make him laugh but it fell down with a clatter. Quick as a flash Jack kicked it so that it rolled out of her reach.

"Miss! Look what Jack's done!" she squealed.

"Dear me!" said Miss Merryday. "You all seem to be in a very fidgety mood." She walked to the back of the classroom, picked up the pencil and put it down on Daisy's table. "I think you'd better all put your books away and we'll go to the Book Corner early today. There's something important that we need to plan together."

The children hurried to put their books in their trays. What does Miss Merryday mean? they wondered.

As soon as everybody was sitting comfortably Miss Merryday said, "It's going to be our turn to take Assembly very soon –"

"I guessed you were going to say that!" said Chantelle, waving her hand in the air.

"That was clever of you!" said Miss

Merryday. "You can put your hand down now, Chantelle. What I want you all to do is to put your thinking caps on. I have been thinking about what we could do and I thought it would be interesting if we talked about people or things that are special to each of us."

"Oh, man!" Jack groaned. He didn't like telling teachers his secret thoughts.

"Don't be silly, Jack," said Miss Merryday. "To help you, I'll tell you what I would choose. It would be my new kitten. She's black all over, except that she has a white tip to her tail. She's got big ears and big eyes and she gets very excited about chasing bits of string. She's very special to me!"

Miss Merryday opened her handbag

and searched for something. At last she pulled out a photograph.

"Here she is! She's called Bramble," she said. She showed the class the photograph, taking it round so that everybody could see.

"The white tip looks as if it's been painted!" Daisy said.

Miss Merryday laughed. "Perhaps one of you has a pet that you would like to tell the others about. Or you might choose a person, or your favourite game – someone or something that makes you feel happy."

Miss Merryday walked round the classroom, coming to each table in turn. "If you can't think of anything yet, just be quiet for the moment. Everybody think

hard! Use your pretend thinking caps," she said.

After a bit she said, "Have you all chosen something? What do you like very much?"

"Ice-cream and jelly," said Mary quickly. Some children giggled. Mary was always eating and talking about food.

"Football," said Mustapha. Jack frowned at him. That was what *he* would have said if he had wanted to join in. But he didn't want to, so instead he looked

over to the window behind Miss Merryday's head and watched the rain pouring down. They wouldn't be able to play out after school. How boring! He didn't want to look at the rain any longer, so he started to listen to what the others were saying.

"My big brother!" said Chantelle.

"Flowers," said Owen. Everyone looked at him because he hardly ever said a word. He turned bright red.

"Owen said 'Flowers'," said Daisy.

"Yes. I heard him perfectly clearly," said Miss Merryday. "Isn't it interesting! We all have such different things and people that are special to us."

"Can we bring in photos, Miss?" Sonia asked. "I've got a good one of my nan."

"Yes," said Miss Merryday. "But it

would be hard for the school to see a small photograph. You might like to copy it and paint a big picture."

"Can we all do our own pictures if we want?" Melodie asked. "I haven't chosen anything special yet but if we can do pictures that will help me to choose," she explained.

"Yes. I would like you all to paint a really big picture – big enough for everyone to see if you hold it up in the Assembly. And afterwards we can put the pictures outside our classroom. We can make a frieze of them and then the rest of the school will see them when they walk past."

"Can two people do the same thing?" Jack asked, frowning. He'd never be able to think of anything better than football and he didn't like to think that Mustapha would be the only one allowed to do that.

"Of course. It's entirely up to you what you choose," said Miss Merryday. "Tomorrow we'll start the pictures. Now if you make yourselves comfortable, I'll carry on with the story we were reading yesterday."

Jack leaned back against the wall. He shut his eyes. He liked to think that Miss Merryday wouldn't know whether he was listening or not. Usually he let his mind wander far away but this story about a little dragon was better than most and he listened to every word.

The next day Miss Merryday gave everybody a very big piece of paper.

Mustapha drew a black and white football and then painted bright green grass all round it. He looked very pleased with his picture.

Jack tried to draw himself in goal but he had a lot of trouble drawing the net.

Sonia drew a big picture of her nan wearing some bright pink slippers.

Chantelle drew herself going to the park with her big brother. "He's much bigger than most grown-ups!" she explained in case anyone thought she had made him too tall.

Everybody was very busy. Now and again they called to Miss Merryday to admire their pictures or to ask her to help them. The only person who didn't do any painting and who didn't ask for help was Owen.

"Owen isn't doing anything," said Daisy.

"Get on with your own work, please," said Miss Merryday. "Let me see what you are doing." She came over to look. "I must say that is very good, Daisy. Your doll looks beautiful!"

Daisy beamed and held up her picture in case anybody else wanted to admire it.

Miss Merryday went to talk with Owen. They had a long talk and then she took his big piece of paper away and gave him a smaller one. By the end of the day Owen had finished his picture. It was very small, right in the middle of the paper.

"Let's have a look!" said Daisy.

Owen held the picture close to his chest but she pulled it away. "Ugh! It looks like wriggling caterpillars!" she said rudely.

But when Miss Merryday saw Owen's picture she said, "How very interesting! You can tell the class about it tomorrow!"

The next day Class 1 practised taking their Assembly. Most of the children wrote down what they were going to say. Then they stuck it on the back of their picture so that when they held the picture up for the others to see they could read the words on the back.

But Owen didn't write anything down. He went very red and wouldn't say anything to the class. He wouldn't even explain what was wrong to Miss Merryday. But she sat down on a chair next to him and said very quietly, "Don't worry about reading or talking in front of the whole school. In a way your picture is a bit small for people to see."

She put her elbows on Owen's desk and looked at him. "Can you think of anything else you could do?" she asked.

Owen nodded his head and whispered something in Miss Merryday's ear.

"What a wonderful idea!" Miss Merryday said, and stood up. "That would be great! I think we'll keep that a secret until the day, shall we, Owen?"

At going-home time, when Owen's father came to collect him, Miss Merryday had a long talk with him and Daisy thought that Owen looked pleased, but she couldn't find out what the plan was. Owen wouldn't say anything.

On the day of Class 1's Assembly everything went well. Everybody showed their picture. They all tried to read loudly and clearly.

Anne-Marie, the new girl, still couldn't speak much English. But she held up a picture of the sun shining on a house. "The sun makes me happy!" she said.

Daisy said, "I like playing with my dolls. This is my favourite." She held up her picture for such a long time that Miss Merryday had to ask her to put it down.

"Thank you for showing us that lovely picture!" she said. "I think your arms will ache if you hold it up too long."

Then Miss Merryday fetched something from behind the piano and gave it to Owen. He stepped forward carefully and held up a cactus in a bowl.

Miss Merryday said, "This plant is called a cactus and it is something very special to Owen. Listen very carefully to what he tells you about it."

"It's more than one hundred years old," Owen said. Then he stopped.

Some teachers and children gasped.

Miss Merryday said, "It is special to Owen because it was his great-grandpa's cactus when he was a little boy such a long, long time ago! Owen told me that most years it has two or three flowers and I think you can all see that it has more than that this year!"

She turned to Owen. "Can you tell everybody how many flowers it has now?" she asked.

"Eight," said Owen. There was a long silence.

He had arranged with Miss Merryday that she would say the next bit but she didn't. He felt himself getting all hot and bothered. In the end he said in a rush, "It's me that's looking after it now, 'cos my grandad died."

Mrs Thompson, the Headteacher, thanked Class 1 warmly.

"I have enjoyed your assembly very much indeed!" she said. "It was a lovely idea for you all to tell us what is special for each of you. And I have learned something most interesting. I know that trees can live for a few hundred years but I had no idea that such a small cactus could live for over a hundred years!"

Some children giggled. They thought that Headteachers knew nearly every-

102

thing and here was something that Mrs Thompson had learned from Owen, the boy in Class 1 who hardly ever spoke a word!

"Nobody is ever too old to learn!" Mrs Thompson said with a smile. "Try and remember that – not just today but even when you have left Nightingale School," she added, looking especially at the oldest children.

Then Mrs Thompson looked at the big clock in the hall. "It's time to go back to your classrooms now," she said. "Miss Merryday has told me that Class 1 will be making a frieze outside their classroom of their pictures so we shall all have a chance to see them again later."

The children began to fidget and to whisper.

Mrs Thompson continued in a louder voice, "But since Owen will have to take his cactus home, perhaps he would be kind enough to stand forward and as you all walk out back to your rooms, you can have a good look at this very special plant."

The children at the front began to get
ready to stand up when their teacher told
them to.

Mrs Thompson continued speaking.
"No touching – just have a good look at
the lovely cactus flowers."

Owen felt his face go all hot again, but he stepped forward and held his cactus so that everybody could see its eight bright red flowers.

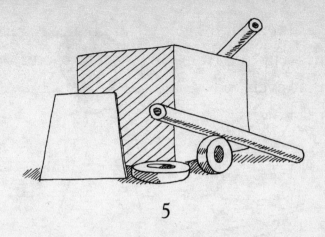

5

Mustapha's News

On Monday morning Mustapha hurried into school. He had not seen Jack at all over the weekend and he had a lot of things he wanted to tell him.

Something very unfair had happened. Mustapha's little cousin had been using Mustapha's special trolley all the weekend, and none of the grown-ups had made him give it back.

"Where's Jack, Miss?" he asked Miss Merryday before she had time to read the register. Jack was never late. His mum always dropped him off at school before she went to work. Mustapha had a feeling inside him that something was wrong.

"I'm afraid Jack has chickenpox. His mother called to tell us," Miss Merryday announced to the class.

Mustapha felt this bad news sink down into a heavy feeling in his stomach, rather like a heavy pudding. He must have looked worried because Miss Merryday came over to him.

"Jack will be away for quite a few days," she said. "If you would like to, you can write him a letter this morning and perhaps you can draw him a picture to cheer him up."

Mustapha fiddled with his shirt collar as he always did when he was bothered. How could he put down in a letter all the things that were bothering him? Even if he could, would Jack be too ill to read them? He didn't want Jack's mum or dad or his older sister to read his private letter.

"Thanks, Miss," he mumbled. He

carried on fiddling with his collar all through Assembly.

When they returned to the classroom, Miss Merryday announced, "I am going to give you all a piece of paper to write a letter to Jack. If you can't think what to write, I suggest that you draw a cheerful picture for him. We shall do that first and our number work next."

Soon the class became quiet. All you could hear was colouring in or rubbing out.

Only Mustapha sat still doing nothing. Miss Merryday came to see why he wasn't working.

"I've only got BAD news! I can't think of anything nice," he said gloomily.

"Well. Try and draw something cheerful," she said to Mustapha, but still he could not think what to draw.

Then he had an idea. "Can I use the computer to write a letter?" he asked. Sometimes he could write much better if he used the computer.

Miss Merryday smiled and said that would be all right.

Two minutes later Miss Merryday lost her smile completely. All Mustapha did was to lift the keyboard off the top of the computer where it had been put, but alas, it slipped out of his hand and CRASHED

down on to the desk, then CRASHED on to the chair. It fell off the chair and landed sticking up on end in the box of computer paper.

Everybody took in a deep breath. Whatever had happened?

Miss Merryday rushed over to rescue the keyboard. "Oh, my goodness! How did you manage to be so CLUMSY?" she

said. "Go back to your place! I shall have to see whether this is broken or not."

Miss Merryday picked the keyboard up very carefully. Mustapha did not stop to watch her. He slipped back to his desk and tried to look invisible. He hoped very much that the computer would not be broken. Enough bad things had happened to him already.

Mustapha was usually a very slow writer, but once he got started his letter to Jack grew quite long. He put:

> You know my trolley
> that I use to unload
> the van-the one like
> my uncle's only it's small.
> Well my little cousin
>   is using it.
>   I wish he had his
> own and not mine.
>   It's not fair!

After all that writing and the shock of the computer crash he felt tired. He had trouble drawing his uncle's van. It did not look good at all. He knew Jack would have done a better picture. He was afraid that nothing about his letter or picture would cheer Jack up.

Everything has gone wrong and that is a rubbish picture! he thought. He nearly crumpled it up to throw it away but Miss Merryday came by and picked up all the letters and began some number work with the class.

They worked quite hard, right until the end of the morning.

Things went much better in the afternoon. Miss Merryday announced that the keyboard still worked and then everyone was allowed to paint or to make a model with cardboard boxes and tubes. For a few days Mustapha and Jack had been waiting for their turn on the brand new building kit.

"Can I build something with that?" he asked, pointing to the new kit, but expecting the answer NO.

However, Miss Merryday said, "Yes. I know you have been waiting for a turn. You can have it all to yourself today. You should be able to make something wonderful with all those pieces!"

Mustapha knelt down and looked at all the pieces. He couldn't believe his luck that he could have all this to himself! First he pulled out the tubes. There were some long ones and middle-size ones. They looked very strong.

Without thinking of a clear plan, he soon had around him all the things he would need to build a trolley. He still had his own trolley at home on his mind – the one he used to unload the van.

He worked very hard. He looked at the two long tubes he had chosen for the main part of the trolley and decided to put two small pieces on them as handles. Then he added a square piece to put the boxes on. Now all he needed were some wheels. He dug deep into the box and there were eight wheels. All he needed were two.

It was a hard task, but eventually Mustapha had made what looked to him like a brilliant trolley. It was bigger than his one at home. He pushed it carefully round the paint table, past the model-builders and wheeled it up to Miss Merryday.

"Look, Miss!" he said shyly. He felt proud too.

"Mustapha! That is just wonderful! You must have worked really hard to do that! I think Mrs Thompson would love to see how clever you have been. Would you like to wheel it to show her?"

Mustapha's toes curled with delight. He had never before been asked to show Mrs Thompson anything. It was what happened only to the very best work. It was usually written work. He didn't think anyone had ever taken a model or anything they had built with the new kit.

Mustapha wheeled his trolley carefully out of the door, along the hall towards Mrs Thompson's room.

He was all ready to say, "Miss Merryday said I could show you this." But to his disappointment he saw that her door was wide open and nobody was in.

"Can I help you?" Miss Smith, the secretary, asked. She had her arms full and was walking out of her room towards the new store room.

"Miss Merryday said I could show this to Mrs Thompson," Mustapha said.

"Sorry, dear. She's not here right now and I can't stop. These boxes are really heavy." And off she went towards the store.

Mustapha did not know what to do. He didn't walk so tall now. When you had something to show Mrs Thompson you walked as tall as you could because it was a good feeling.

He was still standing there when Miss Smith returned.

"My goodness. Did you make that by yourself?" she asked. She bent down to inspect the trolley from the handles down to the wheels. Mustapha showed her proudly and explained how he had made it.

"I shall be sure to tell Mrs Thompson. I think it is wonderful!" she said.

There was nothing more to do, so Mustapha walked slowly back to his classroom.

Miss Merryday wanted to know what Mrs Thompson had said, so he told her that she wasn't there. He knew his voice sounded a bit sad but he couldn't hide his feelings. Jack would have been much more "cool" he knew. He sat around and wondered what to do next. To his relief Miss Merryday clapped her hands.

"I think we shall go to the Book Corner early this afternoon. As soon as you have all finished what you are working on, we'll go. If your model needs to dry, put your name on it and leave it on the table."

Mustapha trailed over to the box that the building kit came in. He couldn't bear to take his trolley to pieces, so he propped it against a cupboard. Then he

heard Miss Merryday call out, "Mustapha, can you bring your wonderful trolley over to the Book Corner? I think everybody would like to see it. It would be good if you told us all how you put it together."

By the time everybody was seated on the carpet in the Book Corner, Mustapha had worked out what he would say about building the trolley, but in the end he did

not need to say a word. Because as soon as Miss Merryday had asked for quiet, in came Mrs Thompson.

"Miss Merryday, Miss Smith told me that Mustapha has something very clever to show me!" she said.

The next minute Mustapha stood up – very tall – and was showing off his trolley. He was quite surprised at Mrs Thompson's reaction. "How wonderful! I

wonder whether Miss Smith and I could borrow Mustapha for a while? A strong trolley like that is exactly what we need to help us move all the things into the new store room!"

Mustapha proudly wheeled his trolley out and he worked very hard all

afternoon. He was good at loading trolleys and this one was very strong. His little cousin could never have moved so many things.

By the end of the afternoon Mustapha had helped Mrs Thompson and Miss Smith to move everything into the new store room. He wondered whether he could ask for a

bigger trolley to use at home and then he could leave the small one for his cousin. He wouldn't mind that at all.

This had been Mustapha's first day at school without Jack.

"I had a bad morning but a great afternoon!" he said to his mum as he left the classroom to go home.

Miss Merryday heard him and she said, "Goodbye, Mustapha! I'm glad you had some GOOD NEWS at last. Come back to Nightingale tomorrow. Let us hope it will be another great day!"

The End